# PAR-TAY!

## DANCE OF THE VEGGIES (AND THEIR FRIENDS)

WRITTEN BY **ELOISE GREENFIELD**

ILLUSTRATIONS BY **DON TATE**

**ALAZAR PRESS**

CARRBORO, NORTH CAROLINA

Text Copyright © 2018 by Eloise Greenfield
Illustration Copyright © 2018 by Don Tate

Library of Congress Control Number: 2017932830
978-0-9977720-2-9 (Hardback)
978-0-9977720-3-6 (eBook)

Edited by Jacqueline Ogburn
Design and production by Richard Hendel

Alazar Press, an imprint of Royal Swan Enterprises, Inc.
www.alazar-press.com

First Edition      Printed in Canada

*To my great-grandsons,*
*Machai and Jalen —E.G.*

*To Avayah Lucille Williams.*
*Eat your veggies, baby girl.*
*And dance! —D.T.*

CLICK

The head of cabbage,
sitting in the fridge,
hears the front door close,
hears the click of the key
turning the lock.

He opens the refrigerator door,
peeps out, then creeps
through the dark rooms to the
front window.

He looks out
and sees, in the moonlight,
his people getting into their car.

Cabbage watches the car pull off,
runs back to the kitchen,
and turns on the light.
He stands in the middle of the floor,
skinny legs and feet apart,
skinny arms high in the air,
throws his head back and yells . . .

Out from the fridge come
the veggies and their friends,
they hear the cabbage calling,
love the message that he sends,
they see the magic instruments
sailing into place,
Eggplant takes the piano,
Basil takes the bass,
Tomato takes the saxophone,
Swiss Chard takes the drum,
they make a mighty music
for the party that's to come.

The others form a circle,
and then begin to sway, they
clap to all the rhythms, dancers
dance in their own way.

First up, Zucchini,
in the center
of the circle.
Zucchini's cool,
lets the music tell him
how to move, what to do.

YEAH!

Showing off, a little bit,
but mostly,
in his head he's far away,
dancing in the world
of the music.

Hip-Hop String Bean,
she is *mean*!
Rippling her arms,
like waves in the ocean,
pumping her knees,
a string bean in motion,
hip-hop,
doing the pop,
hip-hop,
she can't stop,
she can't stop.

"Somebody save me!"
her friends hear her say,
but she's still dancing,
even as Asparagus
is dragging her away.

Whew!
PAR–TAY!

The baby limas wobble-dance,
can hardly stand at all,
their mamas run
and catch them,
the moment they start to fall.

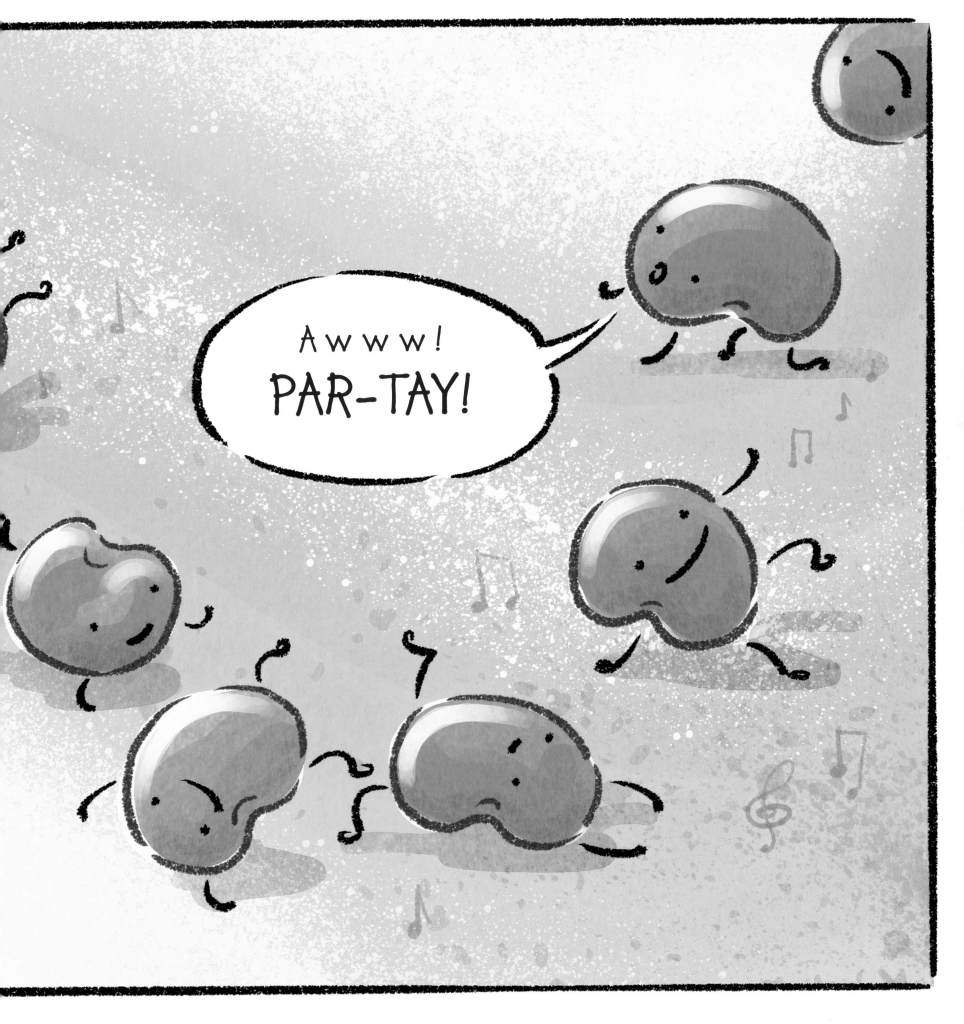

The chili peppers,
right on the beat,
stomping their feet.
They're hot.

ONE...two...three...ON

Mr. Corn and Ms. Arugula
waltz. They
**ONE-two-three,**
**ONE-two-three,**
**ONE-two-three, ONE. . .**
He holds her hand, she dips,
leans, turns,
they long-step walk
to the music, waltz
to the music,
**ONE-two-three,**
**ONE-two-three, ONE . . .**

The sweet potato sisters,
watching from their bin,
waiting, ever-patient,
for their turn to begin.
Then,
the sweet potato sisters
dance as sweet as pie,
pirouette and flit
and flutter,
curtsy with a sigh.

Oh, my!
PAR-TAY!

Artichoke doesn't want to dance,
he is much too shy,
but the other dancers beg him,
and he thinks that he should try.
He keeps his head and shoulders down,
and moves a little bit,
but then he hears his friends all say,

"Go, 'Choke!
Go, 'Choke!
Go, 'Choke!
Go, 'Choke!
You're going to be a hit,"

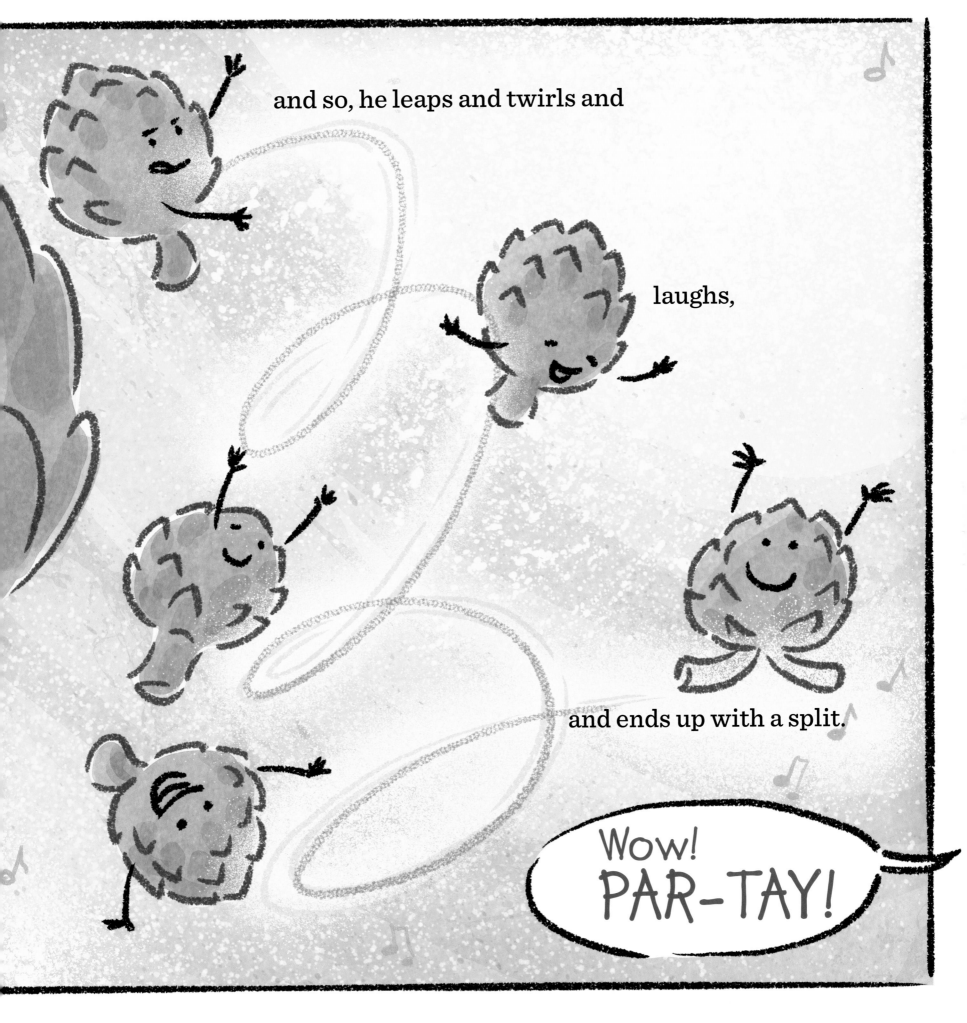

The veggies and their friends
leave the circle,
dance all over the place,
the kale, the collards,
the yellow squash,
etcetera, etcetera, etcetera,
all doing their own thing.
They dance until they tire
and start to sweat.

It's time to stop.
They dance a slow, tired dance
back into the fridge
(sweet potatoes to the bin),
close the door,
and relax in the delicious
coldness, happy with thoughts
of the night and their
fantabulous

PAR-TAY.
YEAHHHH.

# WHAT IS A VEGETABLE?

Not everyone agrees on the answer to this question, but many experts believe that the answer depends on the part of the plant that is being eaten. The leaves (e.g. spinach), the stem (e.g. celery), the flower (e.g. broccoli) and the root (e.g. carrots) are all vegetables. The part of the plant that contains seeds is a fruit.

Some fruits, such as tomatoes and eggplants are used as vegetables. Tomatoes, for example, are often eaten with vegetables in salads, or on a sandwich with lettuce, or cooked with vegetables.  People rarely hold a tomato in their hands and take a bite, as they do with other small fruits, such as apples and pears.

There are some exceptions to the distinction between vegetables and fruits.  Corn is a fruit (and also a grain), but we don't eat the cob— the part that holds the seeds. We eat the seeds only. With string beans and some other fruits, we eat the seeds *and* the part that holds them. Seedless grapes are another exception. They are fruit, but scientists have figured out a way to grow them without seeds.

It's all a bit hard to understand, but what do we care, as long as these foods taste good and are good for us? And some night when we're not at home, our foods might decide to throw a partay,  and if we sneak back home at the right time, we can  catch them dancing all over the place.

Here, in order of their appearance in this book, are the veggie characters and their friends:

*Veggies*:  Cabbage, Basil, Swiss Chard, Asparagus, Ms. Arugula, the sweet potato sisters, Artichoke, the kale and the collards.

*Fruits*:  Eggplant, Tomato, Zucchini, Hip-Hop String Bean, the baby limas, their mamas, the chili peppers, Mr. Corn and the yellow squash.

*Eloise Greenfield*

## REFERENCES

Buckingham, Alan, Jo Whittingham. *Grow Vegetables.*
New York: Dorling Kindersley Limited, 2008.

Schneider, Elizabeth. *Vegetables from Amaranth to Zucchini: The Essential Reference.* New York: William Morrow, 2001.

"Vegetables." Encyclopedia Britannica Online.
Encyclopedia Britannica, Inc. 2012.
*http://www.britannica.com/EBchecked/topic/624564/vegetable*
17 July 2012.